*This is a story about kindness*
*that I learned from Moritz.*

# An Open Heart

A Story About Moritz by
Barry J. Schieber

Illustrated by
Hedvig Rappe-Flowers

Silent Moon Books

Dedication

*To the kindness in each of us.*

Acknowledgement to Hedvig Rappe-Flowers

*For her skill and understanding in translating the spirit of the book into her illustrations. And for her courage in her personal life.*

Silent Moon Books

Post Office Box 1865
Bigfork, Montana 59911

Orders and information

info@silentmoonbooks.com

A portion of the proceeds from the sale of *An Open Heart*
will be donated to animal welfare projects.

"Wake up, Moritz, we're going for a hike to Pyramid Lake," Barry says as he rubs my head early one summer morning. Moments later, we are in the car heading up the mountain to the trail. We pull into an empty parking lot, find a place to park, and I jump to the ground.

The day-old smell of packhorses tickles my nose. While Barry puts on his hiking boots and his backpack, I rush to the trailhead leading to the Bob Marshall Wilderness.

ENTERING
BOB MARSHALL
WILDERNESS

The sun has just risen. The forest is misty, the air fresh and full of pine scent and birdsong. Excited and happy, I run back to Barry and squeeze between his legs.

We start up the trail. I race ahead on a broad path covered with pine needles and bordered with pine and Douglas fir. I'm careful – I know if I go too far off the trail or run too far ahead, I'm sure to hear Barry calling out, "Moritz!"

Squirrels and chipmunks are gathering nuts and pinecones. When they see me, they scurry up trees or into ground holes, but I hardly ever chase them.

I slow down to walk along with Barry, listening to the quiet forest. The path narrows and enters a meadow filled with the tall white flowering cones of bear grass. Butterflies flit among alpine flowers – red, blue, yellow, and white. We follow a small creek through the meadow and then begin to climb up the mountainside.

It's warmer now and after awhile we stop beside a spring.
I take a long, cool drink and Barry sits down and reaches into
his backpack for a treat for me. Gently I take it from his hand.
A few noisy crunches and it's gone. We rest in silence.

From here the trail rises, narrow and rocky, alongside a
mountain stream. Higher up, the soft gurgle of bubbling water
deepens into a low roar as the stream gushes over a waterfall
and sprays mist onto the trail.

We pause to look at the delicate bright green moss on the
rocks and stream banks.

I wade into the water chest deep to cool off. Then I slowly lie down. . . . Ahhh.

Refreshed, I shake the water from my coat. We begin climbing again, carefully making our way up and up.

We reach a high plateau overlooking a pass between the mountains. It is very quiet. We listen to the wind blowing through the trees. I look at Barry and walk over to sit beside him.

Then, while he checks the map, I go exploring. He calls me, and we turn off the trail onto a small path that crosses streams and leads to a rise overlooking Pyramid Lake.

We walk down and sit on a large rock. Barry gets out his thermos and pours himself a cup of tea; he gives me a treat and unpacks our lunch – including cheese for me. We Swiss dogs love cheese.

We watch ripples blow across the lake. Under a deep blue sky, Pyramid Mountain still has some snow. I lay my head on Barry's leg. He gently puts his hand on my neck and we seem to melt into space.

Deer appear on the other shore, but we don't see other people or even horses. Birds fly overhead, we barely move. A marmot chirps and I sit up. I like to chase marmots, but not today.

Afternoon sunlight slants through the trees as we stand up and start back home. We hike down a different path – an old, rugged Indian trail that's seldom used. There are hundreds of flowers among the rocks. I can run fast down steep trails, but Barry is more careful and takes his time. I often run ahead and then come back to check on him. Sometimes I just sit or lie down on the trail to wait for him.

I stop for another cool drink, and then race past him down the path and around the side of the mountain.

This time it takes awhile for Barry to catch up. He walks around the bend just in time to see a large doe looking down on the trail from the slope above. The sunlight makes her tawny coat glow. He stops and stares at her.

Then he looks back at me. I am sitting next to a small brown lump. He squints to try and make out what it is. From where he stands, perhaps it looks like a small stump or log, or maybe a backpack lying on the trail.

As he comes nearer, he sees it is a baby deer – a fawn, hunkered down, dead still.

Barry looks alarmed. "Moritz," he says, "did you hurt the fawn?"

With my nose, I nudge her again and again. Her big brown eyes are wide open; she does not move.

Barry asks, "Moritz, did you kill the fawn?"

His voice is stern. He shouts at me to walk away. I obey, and Barry orders: "Sit!"

As I look up at him, the fawn
leaps up and runs to her mother.

Barry is so surprised! He hugs me and says, "I'm sorry, Moritz. I thought you hurt the fawn. But you only wanted to play."

He sits down on a rock.

Suddenly, he begins to cry.

I nudge him with my nose and lick his face. He draws me close, unable to stop crying.

"Moritz," he tells me, "in this world, human beings kill each other every day. We have such a hard time living in peace. Yet you are always kind to everyone.

"Oh Moritz, thank you. You show me how easy it is to be kind when you have an open heart."

## About the Author

Barry J. Schieber continues the inspiring stories of his companion and friend Moritz, a large Bernese Mountain Dog. His books about Moritz, *A Gift to Share* and *Nose to Nose,* have won the hearts of children and adults throughout the world.

## About the Illustrator

Hedvig Rappe-Flowers lives in Bozeman, Montana, with her two Nordic skier daughters, equally fantastic husband, and Springer Spaniel. She has illustrated the children's book *Spotted Bear*, designed posters, painted life-size grizzly bears and mountain sheep for community fund-raising projects, and created a myriad of artistic pieces over the last twenty years. Currently she is an artist in residence at Bozeman Elementary Schools.